Scruff
and the Goat

Illustrations by Nigel Chilvers

EGMONT

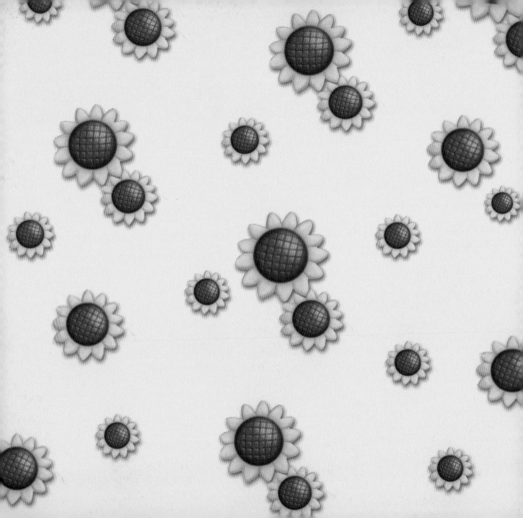

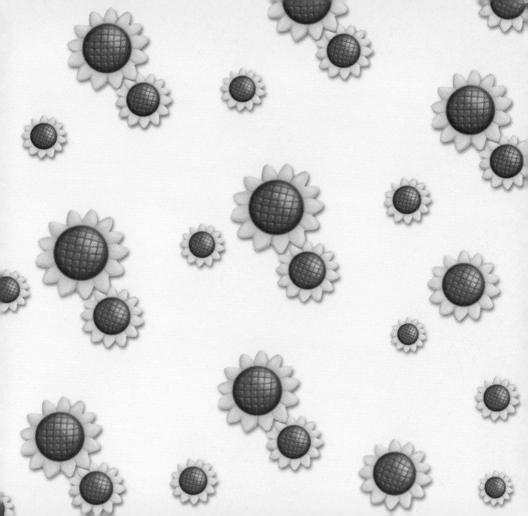

EGMONT

We bring stories to life

First published in Great Britain 2009
by Egmont UK Limited,
239 Kensington High Street, London W8 6SA
Endpapers and introductory illustrations by Craig Cameron.

HiT entertainment

ISBN 978 1 4052 4626 2

1 3 5 7 9 10 8 6 4 2

Printed in Italy

FSC
Mixed Sources
Product group from well-managed
forests and other controlled sources
Cert no. TT-COC-002332
www.fsc.org
© 1996 Forest Stewardship Council

Egmont is passionate about helping to preserve the world's remaining ancient forests.
We only use paper from legal and sustainable forest sources.

This book is made from paper certified by the Forestry Stewardship Council (FSC),
an organisation dedicated to promoting responsible management of forest resources.
For more information on the FSC, please visit www.fsc.org. To learn more about
Egmont's sustainable paper policy, please visit www.egmont.co.uk/ethical

Travis and Scruffty are in such a hurry, they lose Farmer Pickles' goat, Giddy. Will they be able to find her and bring her safely to Sunflower Valley?

One day, Bob had a new job for the team – they were going to build a goat run at Farmer Pickles' farm. "A goat run is a big climbing frame … for goats!" Bob said.

But the machines were puzzled – there weren't any goats on Farmer Pickles' farm!

"Travis and Scruffty are collecting our first goat now," explained Farmer Pickles. "She's called Giddy. We'll use her wool to make warm scarves and jumpers."

Scruffty bounced along in the trailer as Travis raced along the road. It was a bumpy ride!

Soon they arrived at the Old Farm in Bobsville. Meg MacDonald was there to meet them with Giddy the goat.

"Hello, Giddy! We've come to take you to Sunflower Valley!" said Travis.

"Drive carefully, Travis!" warned Meg, as she led Giddy in to the trailer.

With the goat safely on board, Travis set off back to Sunflower Valley. "Hang on to your horns, Giddy!" he called.

But Travis was going too fast. Suddenly, he hit a bump in the road. Travis slammed on his brakes but the trailer door flew open and the goat jumped out.

"Ruff, ruff!" barked Scruffty, as Giddy clip-clopped away into the bushes.

"Giddy! Come back!" Travis wailed.

Meanwhile, Bob and the team were hard at work building the goat run.

"That's the first level finished!" smiled Wendy, proudly.

Bob looked up from his plans to see that a sheep had climbed on top of the goat run.

"Baaaa!" went the sheep.

"What are you doing up there?" Bob chuckled. "This goat run is for Giddy. She'll be here soon with Scruffty and Travis!"

Back in the woods, Scruffty and Travis couldn't find Giddy anywhere.

Travis was worried. "I need your help, Scruffty," he said. "Can you find Giddy's trail to follow?"

Scruffty put his nose to the ground and began to sniff. He soon picked up someone's trail, but it wasn't Giddy's …

"Spud!" cried Travis, as Spud the Scarecrow jumped out from behind a tree.

"Hello, you two!" Spud beamed.

Travis told Spud all about how they had lost Giddy. "We've got to find her," he worried.

"Ruff!" nodded Scruffty.

"Don't worry, I'll help you," said Spud. "I'll be Spud the Goat-finder!"

So the great goat hunt began!

At the site, more of Farmer Pickles' animals wanted a go on the goat run. There were hens, rabbits, cows and sheep!

"It looks like we've got a little problem here!" said Bob, scratching his head.

"We'll have to build a bigger run, for all the animals to share," Wendy suggested.

"Good idea! Can we build it?" asked Bob.
"Yes, we can!" the machines replied.
"Er, yeah, I think so," added Lofty.

Travis and Spud searched all over for Giddy. They tried making bleating noises, but the missing goat was nowhere to be seen.

"Where are you, Giddy?" Travis called.

Suddenly, there came a small "Beh!" from over the hill. Scruffty pricked up his ears. Travis and Spud heard it, too.

"Jump in my trailer!" Travis told Scruffty and Spud. "We'll follow that bleat!"

With everyone on board, Travis raced away.

"There she is!" shouted Travis. He revved his engine and clattered between two trees, chasing after Giddy the goat.

"Slow down, Travis!" warned Spud.

Suddenly, the trailer bashed into a rock. Travis screeched to a stop but one of the trailer wheels came off!

"Oh, no! First, I lost Giddy and now I've broken the trailer," said Travis sadly. "What am I going to tell Farmer Pickles?"

While Travis and Scruffty stopped to think, Spud wandered off into the bushes.

A little while later, Spud came back . . . with Giddy munching on the end of his scarf!

"I can't believe it!" cried Travis. "As soon as we stopped rushing, she turned up!"

"Now all we have to do is get Giddy to her goat run!" said Spud. "But how?"

Scruffty had a clever idea. "Ruff!" he barked, tugging on the other end of Spud's scarf.

"That's it!" cried Spud. "We'll use my scarf to lead Giddy home! Well done, Scruffty!"

"Next stop is your new goat run, Giddy! And this time I'll go *very slowly*!" Travis promised.

Scruffty led the way, with Spud and Travis following behind with Giddy.

They arrived at the site to find all sorts of animals on the goat run.

"Meet Giddy the goat!" Spud announced.

"Welcome to the farm, Giddy!" said Bob. "We hope you like your goat run."

At the top, there was just enough room for Giddy and Scruffty to squeeze on. "Ruff!" went Scruffty, and "Beh!" went Giddy.

"It looks like Giddy and Scruffty are best friends already!" smiled Wendy.

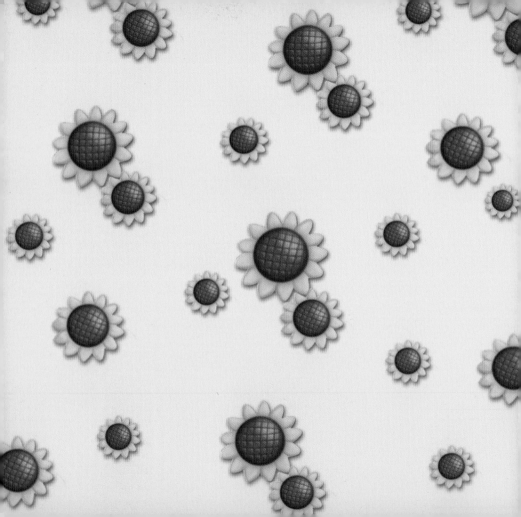

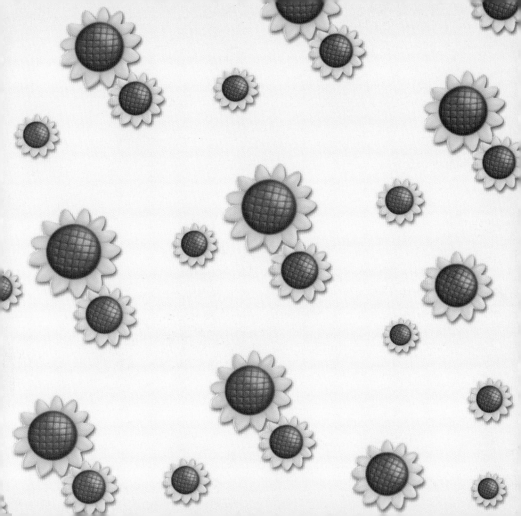

Start collecting your Bob the Builder Story Library NOW!

Bob and the Big Plan ①

Dizzy and the Talkie-Talkie ②

Scrambler and the Off-road Race ③

Wendy and the Surprise Party ④

Roley and the Woodland Walk ⑤

Benny and the Important Job ⑥

Sumsy and the Sunflower Spill ⑦

Muck and the Machine Convoy ⑧

Travis and the Tropical Fruit ⑨

Lofty and the Singing Stars ⑩

Scoop and the Bakery Build ⑪

Spud and the Funny Trees ⑫

Packer and the Difficult Day ⑬

Dodger and the Dairy Delivery ⑭

Pilchard and the Big Surprise ⑮

Tumbler and the Skate Park ⑯

Gripper, Grabber and the Sports Stadium ⑰

Scruffty and the Goat Hunt ⑱

Flex and the Fix-it Day ⑲

Bristle and the Big Clean ⑳

'Bob Goodies Please' Reply Card

Yes I have enclosed 4 special Bob Tokens so please send me a FREE Bob the Builder poster and door hanger ☐ (tick here)

Simply fill in your details below and send this page to:
BOB OFFERS, PO BOX 715, HORSHAM RH12 5WG

To be completed by an adult

Fan's name:
....

Address:
....
....

Postcode:
....

Email:
....

Date of birth:
....

Name of parent / guardian:
....

Signature of parent / guardian:
....

Ref: BOB 006